P9-BZB-735

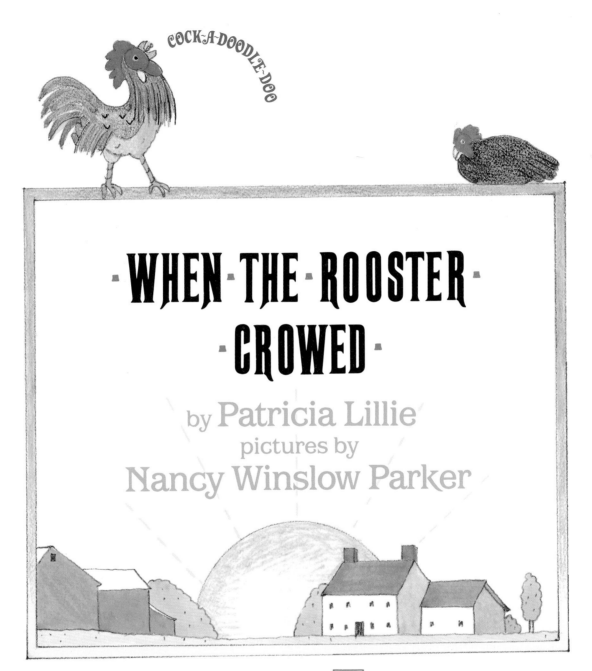

COCK-A-DOODLE-DOO

WHEN·THE·ROOSTER·CROWED·

by Patricia Lillie
pictures by
Nancy Winslow Parker

Greenwillow Books New York

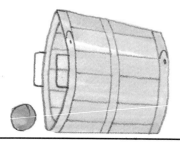

Black pen, watercolor paints, and colored pencils were used for the full-color
art. The text type is Barcelona Medium. Text copyright © 1991 by Patricia Lillie.
Illustrations copyright © 1991 by Nancy Winslow Parker. All rights reserved. No
part of this book may be reproduced or utilized in any form or by any means,
electronic or mechanical, including photocopying, recording, or by any
information storage and retrieval system, without permission in writing from
the Publisher, Greenwillow Books, a division of William Morrow
& Company, Inc., 1350 Avenue of the Americas, New York, NY 10019.
Printed in U.S.A. by Brighter Vision Inc.
Reprinted by permission of Greenwillow Books, a division of
William Morrow & Co. Inc.

Library of Congress Cataloging-in-Publication Data
Lillie, Patricia.
When the rooster crowed/by Patricia Lillie;
pictures by Nancy Winslow Parker.
p.   cm.
Summary: Not until all his animals join voices
is a farmer able to get out of bed in the morning.
ISBN 0-688-09378-7.   ISBN 0-688-09379-5 (lib. bdg.)
[1. Farm life—Fiction.   2. Domestic animals—Fiction.
3. Animal sounds—Fiction.]   I. Nancy Winslow Parker, ill.
II. Title.   PZ7.L632Ro   1991
[E]—dc20   90-30783   CIP AC

FOR MOM AND DAD
—P. L.

FOR SELMA LANES
—N. W. P.

When the sun came over the hill,
the rooster crowed, "Cock-a-doodle-doo!"

"Ten more minutes,"
said the farmer.

When the cow said, "Mmmooo,"
the rooster crowed, "Cock-a-doodle-doo!"

"Five more minutes,"
said the farmer.

When the horse went, "Neigh,"
the rooster crowed, "Cock-a-doodle-doo!"

"Just a few more minutes,"
said the farmer.

When the pigs went, "Oink, Oink,"
the rooster crowed, "Cock-a-doodle-doo!"

"One more minute,"
said the farmer.

When the chickens said, "Cluck, Cluck, Cluck,"
the rooster crowed, "Cock-a-doodle-doo!"

"Half a minute,"
said the farmer.

When the farmer's wife yelled, "ALBERT!"
the rooster crowed, "Cock-a-doodle-doo!"

"In a second,"
said the farmer.

But when the cow said,

"MMMOOO,"

CAW

NEIGH

and the horse said,
"NEIGH!"

and the pigs said,
"OINK, OINK,"

and the chickens said,
"CLUCK, CLUCK, CLUCK,"

NEIGH

CAW

OINK

and the farmer's wife yelled, "**ALBERT!**"

and the rooster crowed,

"COCK-A-DOODLE-DOO,"

all at the same time . . .

the farmer said, **"ALL RIGHT!"**

He jumped out of bed,

pulled on his clothes,

milked the cow,

fed the horse,

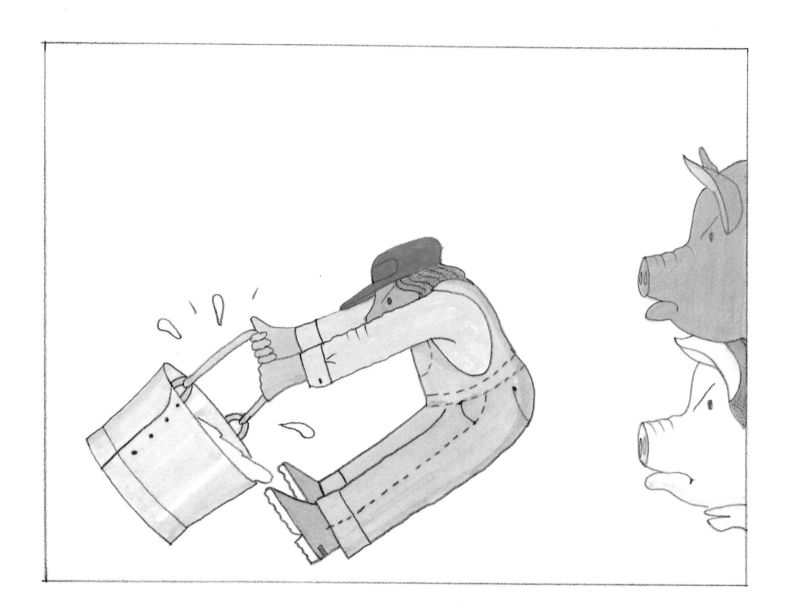

slopped the pigs,

gathered the eggs,

and

sat down for breakfast.